WHERE'S HELLO KITTY?
Fun in the City

First published in the UK by HarperCollins *Children's Books* in 2014

1 3 5 7 9 10 8 6 4 2

ISBN: 978-0-00-753106-6

How to play

No matter where Hello Kitty goes, she's always a trend setter! Lots of other girls copy the way she looks. That's why it can sometimes be hard to pick the real Hello Kitty out in the crowd!

Take a look at the big picture at the top of each page, then see if you can find the real Hello Kitty in the scene. Make sure you really do have the right Hello Kitty before moving on to the next puzzle.

Looking chic in paris

A rainy day in London

Jogging in New York

You'll find lots of other fun activities throughout the book!

Hello Kitty doesn't like to travel alone, so see if you can find her friends in each scene, too! You can also spot Hello Kitty's suitcase – if you look hard enough!

Dear Daniel

Thomas

Fifi

Tippy

Jodie

Moley

Rory

Mimmy
(wears her bow on the opposite side)

Joey

Tracy

Timmy and Tammy

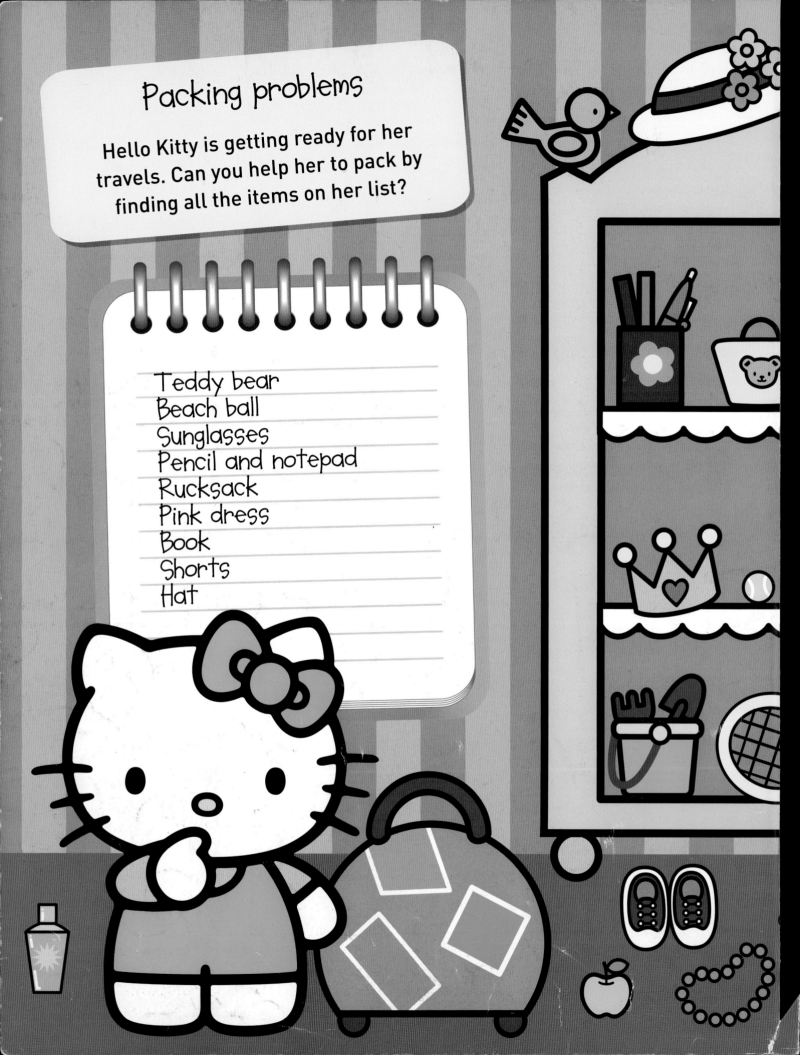

Packing problems

Hello Kitty is getting ready for her travels. Can you help her to pack by finding all the items on her list?

Teddy bear
Beach ball
Sunglasses
Pencil and notepad
Rucksack
Pink dress
Book
Shorts
Hat

I love London!

Where's Hello Kitty?

Hello Kitty is in her home town, London! She's having lots of fun looking at all the sights.

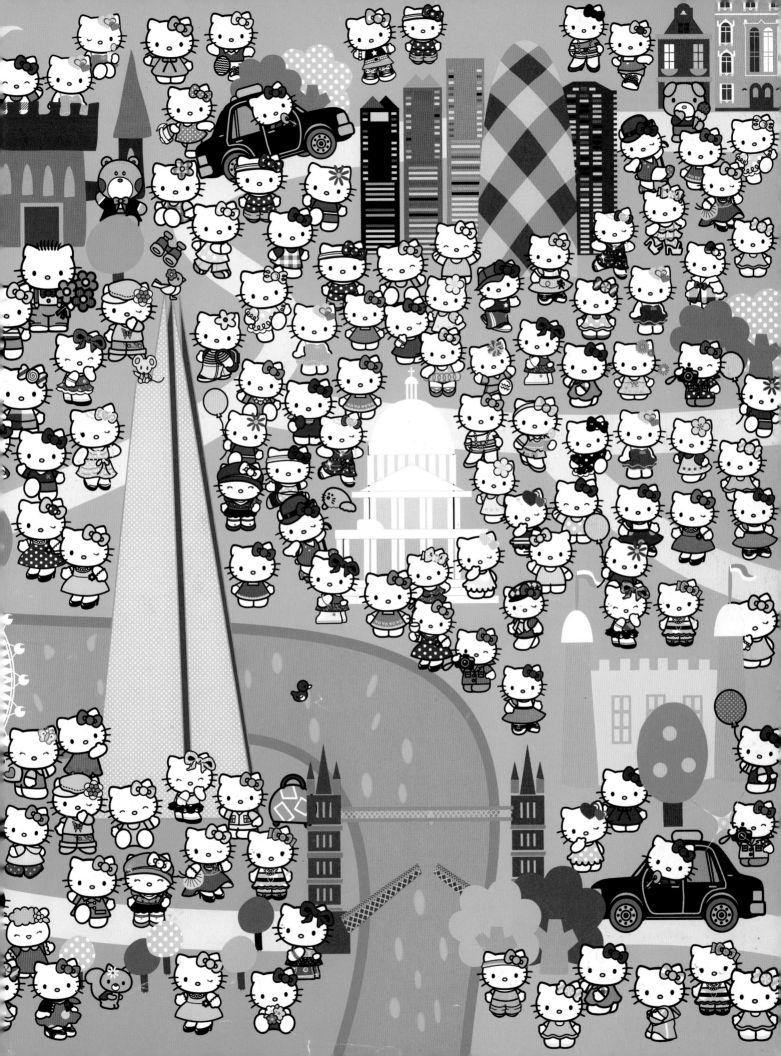

Lost in London

Oh dear, Hello Kitty is a bit lost!
Can you guide her through
the maze to help her
find the bus stop?

Bus tour

Where's Hello Kitty?

One of the best ways to see the sights of London is on an open-top bus! As you can see, they are very popular!

TELEPHONE

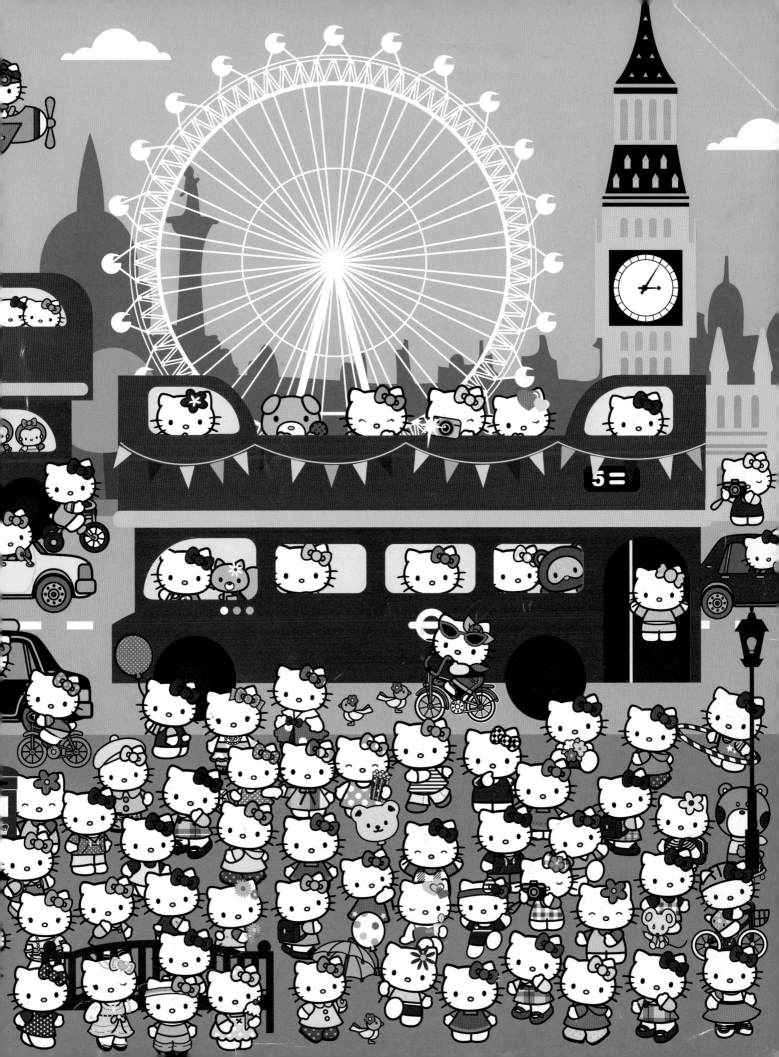

Oui, oui Paris!

Where's Hello Kitty?

Hello Kitty is in the most fashionable city on the planet! But where is she? Is she sipping a hot chocolate at a pavement café or shopping at a chic boutique?

Front row fashion!

Where's Hello Kitty?

Hello Kitty has been invited to an exclusive catwalk show! Everyone is very fashionable, but can you find the very stylish Hello Kitty?

Vive la différence!

Art galleries are super-interesting places to wander around. Can you spot 10 differences between these two pictures?

New York, New York!

Where's Hello Kitty?

Get your shopping bags at the ready, Hello Kitty's in New York! Full of beautiful buildings, incredible shops and yummy delis, what will Hello Kitty do first?

Shop, til you drop!

Oops! Hello Kitty and Mimmy have been to so many shops, their bags have become mixed up! Can you work out which bags belong to Hello Kitty and which belong to Mimmy?

Park life!

Where's Hello Kitty?

New York has a beautiful park in the middle of it. Perfect for resting your feet after a busy day of sightseeing!

Hello Tokyo!

Where's Hello Kitty?

Tokyo is one of the most exciting places in the world! Hello Kitty feels right at home in this colourful city.

ハローキティ

ハローキティ

ハローキティ

Say what?

Japanese is one of the trickiest languages to learn. Use Hello Kitty's dictionary to work out what her new friends are saying.

こんにちは

Tracy is saying Hello

はい

Thomas is saying yes

いいえ

Tammy is saying No

さようなら

Fifi is saying Goodbye

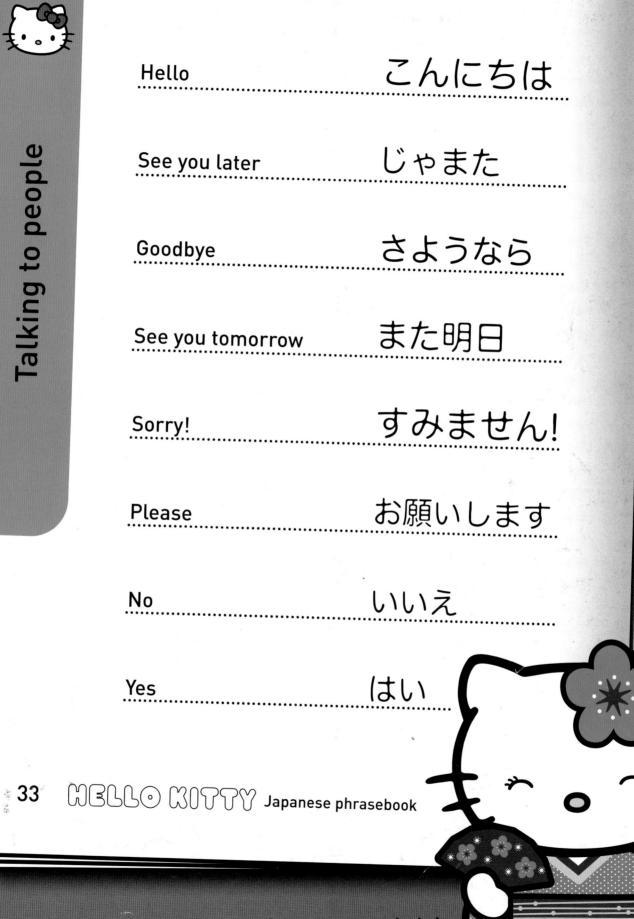

Hello	こんにちは
See you later	じゃまた
Goodbye	さようなら
See you tomorrow	また明日
Sorry!	すみません!
Please	お願いします
No	いいえ
Yes	はい

HELLO KITTY Japanese phrasebook

Have a go at writing one of these Japanese symbols!

Cherry blossom

Where's Hello Kitty?

Springtime in Tokyo is a magical season. The cherry blossom trees come into full bloom and turn the city pink!

Photo memories!

Now Hello Kitty is back from her travels, she's made a photo album of her adventures. Can you spot everything from the list in these pictures?

- 2 yellow ducks
- 5 bicycles
- The Eiffel Tower
- 2 flowers in a vase
- 6 yellow taxis
- A hot air balloon
- 3 fireworks exploding
- 2 butterflies

What else?

Take a look back through this exciting book and see if you can spot these extra images in the crowd scenes!

Binoculars

A green watering can

A cup of tea

A pair of cowboy boots

An orange envelope

A pink peg

A teddy bear

A cupcake